At lunch, we talked about Miss Mackle's wedding in the cafeteria while Harry and ZuZu were in the hot lunch line getting tacos.

"I was hoping Miss Mackle might use an Elvis song in her wedding," Dexter said, waving his cheese stick in the air. "'Love Me Tender' would be perfect. Now I'll never know."

"Well, I'm crushed," Mary replied, chomping into her tuna sandwich. "I wish I had written about how it feels not to get an invitation to your favorite teacher's wedding. Maybe Miss Mackle would have changed her mind and invited us."

"Hey, guys! Why the gloom and doom?" Harry said, joining our table. "I k̶̶̶̶̶̶̶̶̶̶̶ dding."

Other Books by Suzy Kline

Horrible Harry in Room 2B
Horrible Harry and the Green Slime
Horrible Harry and the Ant Invasion
Horrible Harry's Secret
Horrible Harry and the Christmas Surprise
Horrible Harry and the Kickball Wedding
Horrible Harry and the Dungeon
Horrible Harry and the Purple People
Horrible Harry and the Drop of Doom
Horrible Harry Moves Up to Third Grade
Horrible Harry Goes to the Moon
Horrible Harry at Halloween
Horrible Harry Goes to Sea
Horrible Harry and the Dragon War
Horrible Harry and the Mud Gremlins
Horrible Harry and the Holidaze
Horrible Harry and the Locked Closet
Horrible Harry and The Goog
Horrible Harry Takes the Cake
Horrible Harry and the Triple Revenge
Horrible Harry Cracks the Code
Horrible Harry Bugs the Three Bears
Horrible Harry and the Dead Letters
Horrible Harry on the Ropes
Horrible Harry Goes Cuckoo
Horrible Harry and the Secret Treasure
Horrible Harry and the June Box
Horrible Harry and the Scarlet Scissors
Horrible Harry and the Stolen Cookie
Horrible Harry and the Missing Diamond
Horrible Harry and the Hallway Bully
Horrible Harry and the Top-Secret Hideout

HORRIBLE HARRY
and the Wedding Spies

BY **SUZY KLINE**

PICTURES BY **AMY WUMMER**

PUFFIN BOOKS

PUFFIN BOOKS
An imprint of Penguin Random House LLC
375 Hudson Street
New York, New York 10014

First published in the United States of America by Viking,
an imprint of Penguin Young Readers Group, 2015
Published by Puffin Books, an imprint of Penguin Random House LLC, 2016

Text copyright © 2015 by Suzy Kline
Illustrations copyright © 2015 by Penguin Group (USA) Inc.

THE LIBRARY OF CONGRESS HAS CATALOGED THE VIKING EDITION AS FOLLOWS:
Kline, Suzy.
Horrible Harry and the wedding spies / by Suzy Kline ; illustrated by Amy
Wummer.
Pages cm—(Horrible Harry ; 32)
Summary: "When Harry and his pals in Room 3B aren't invited to their
teacher's wedding, they invite themselves, and wind up saving the day"
—Provided by publisher.
ISBN 978-0-670-01552-8 (hardcover)
[1. Weddings—Fiction. 2. Teachers—Fiction. 3. Schools—Fiction.
4. Behavior—Fiction.] I. Wummer, Amy, illustrator II. Title.
PZ7.K6797Hnst 2015 [Fic]—dc23 2014024551

Puffin Books ISBN 978-0-14-750968-0

Printed in the United States of America

1 3 5 7 9 10 8 6 4 2

For Rufus, the love of my life

Special appreciation to . . .

my sharp editor, Leila Sales, whose good questions and thoughtful comments greatly helped me write this book; my copy editor, Janet Pascal, for her critical eye and important contributions; Kitty Penton for going up in our church belfry and taking pictures for me; her husband, Elmer, for spotting the wooden owl up there; Midge and Rod for their valuable help; Bob Bittner, who shared his wonderful pictures of our church bell and belfry with me; Emily and Victor, and Jennifer and Matt for their beautiful weddings; and my husband, Rufus, who read many of my drafts.

Contents

A Ride with Harry   1

Mary's Bad News   6

Something Hard to Do   11

Harry's Horrible Plan   20

The Church Cemetery   30

Flower Baskets   36

Disaster in the Balcony   41

Trapped in the Belfry   51

The Wedding Surprise   57

A Ride with Harry

Usually my friend Harry gets a ride to school with his grandma in her red truck. Monday was different.

"Thanks for the lift, Doug," he said, getting into my mom's car. "My grandma is busy baking a carrot cake this morning."

"No problem," I replied. "What happened to your thumb?"

Harry looked down at his Band-Aid.

"I was grating carrots for her, and I cut myself. Want to see how bloody it is?"

"No, thanks." I cringed.

Harry lowered his voice. "I wonder if I got any skin in Grandma's cake batter."

"Eweyee!" I replied.

Harry cackled. He loves horrible things!

As Mom turned the corner, I could see the tall steeple on my church. Harry was looking at it too.

"Have you ever been up in your church bell tower?" he asked.

"Yeah," I answered. "Just last summer. Mom and I put a wooden owl up there to scare away the pigeons."

"Cool!" Harry exclaimed. "Hey look, Dougo! Your church has a cemetery in the back. We should check out those gravestones on Saturday."

"Saturday? How perfect!" Mom interrupted. "Then you two could join me in our Fellowship Hall and arrange flower bouquets. I need some good helpers. I'll be there all day, so you could stop by whenever you liked."

Harry and I exchanged a look.

Arrange flower bouquets? That was deadly!

"Nooo thank you," we said.

As soon as Mom pulled up at South School, I grabbed my book bag and jumped out of the car. "See you later, Mom!" I called. We ran down the ramp onto the playground. Mary madly waved us over right away. She was standing with Song Lee, Ida, ZuZu, Dexter, and Sidney by the Dumpster.

Mary looked like her cat had died.

"I've been waiting to say this until we were all together. I have some bad news to share . . ."

Mary's Bad News

"What's the bad news?" ZuZu asked.

Mary lowered her voice. "Miss Mackle is getting married on Saturday."

Ida and Song Lee immediately started jumping up and down. They were cheering and clapping.

"That's not bad news," Harry said.

Mary held up a hand. "Wait, there's a part B."

Everyone huddled up again and listened.

"We're not invited!"

All of us were stunned.

"What a bummer!" Harry groaned. "Miss Mackle's my favorite teacher."

"Mine too," Song Lee and Ida chimed in.

"Listen to this," Mary said. "I even got a special pink taffeta dress with red roses on it to wear to Miss Mackle's wedding. I knew it was sometime this spring. I thought for sure she'd invite her class."

"How do you know all this stuff?" ZuZu asked.

"Miss Mackle and my mom go to the same beauty salon—Lucy's Locks. Mom got the scoop last Saturday from Lucy."

Sidney started to whine. "Why didn't she invite us? I thought she liked us."

"Because it's a family only wedding," Mary explained.

"That's not fair," Ida replied. "We're her Room 3B family."

"Where's she getting married?" ZuZu asked.

"Maplewood Church," Mary answered.

"No kidding!" I said. "That's my church!"

"Miss Mackle is getting married this Saturday at Doug's church?" Harry asked. "What time?"

"Noon," Mary answered. "Why?"

Harry paused for a moment and then smiled. "You guys want to arrange flower bouquets on Saturday?"

"Huh?" everyone replied.

"I'll tell you all the details at lunch." Then Harry winked at me.

Oh man! I thought. Harry was hatching a horrible plan!

Something Hard to Do

When we got to Room 3B, Mary brightened up. "Oh, Miss Mackle!" she exclaimed. "I love your new hairdo!" The topic of hairstyling seemed to lift Mary's mood. "Your curls are so pretty," she said.

Miss Mackle looked embarrassed. She put both hands on her face and shook her head. "Thank you, Mary, but I think it's too curly."

"Perms are like that at first," Mary replied.

At ten o'clock, we had writers' workshop. As usual, Miss Mackle wrote a prompt on the board and we had fifteen minutes to write about it. I liked today's topic: Write about something that was hard for you to do.

Everyone got busy writing, even the teacher. I knew what was hard for me—getting along with my annoying brother, Baxter.

When we were done, Miss Mackle got out our portable microphone and passed it to Song Lee, who was sitting in the front row. Everyone looked up and listened while Song Lee read.

"When I came to America, at the end of kindergarten, I spoke just a little English. It was hard for me to learn a new language. I had to go to an ELL class. That means you are an English language learner. I made a lot of mistakes in first and second grade. I kept forgetting to use a, an, and the, and add -s and -ed on my words. It bothered me and kept me from speaking in front of the class. Now, I speak English fine, because I had a wonderful ELL teacher, but I still don't like speaking in front of the class."

Miss Mackle put her hand over her heart. "It is very hard to learn a new language. But you have learned it beautifully! I'm so proud of you."

Song Lee smiled, then passed the microphone to Harry.

"Go ahead," the teacher said.

"High places give me the heebie-jeebies. If you don't know what those are, maybe you know about the screaming meemies, willies, butterflies in your stomach, or jitters. Same thing. When I have to ride an elevator, I freak out. I start sweating, get goose pimples, and my stomach is like a washing machine on the spin cycle. But I am working on it. I actually made it to the top of the climbing rope in gym. I rode the Drop of Doom at Mountainside Park too, but I had to be really psyched to do it." When Harry glanced over at Song Lee, I knew what he was thinking. She was his inspiration. "Mostly, I just avoid high places."

"You tell it the way it is, Harry, and use lots of detail," said Miss Mackle. "That's good writing!"

Harry beamed.

Sidney took a turn next. "I don't like being left out. That's very hard. Every time someone passes out birthday invitations, I wait to get mine. Sometimes I don't get a birthday invitation. Then I want to cry and shout, 'Give me a birthday invitation!'"

It was very quiet when Sid finished. I knew where he got the idea to write about that.

Miss Mackle's wedding!

"I feel the same way you do, Sidney," the teacher said. "That's why I don't allow anyone to pass out invitations in class. That should be private. Thank you for sharing, Sidney. I love the feeling you put into your writing."

After we passed the microphone around the room, it finally ended up on the teacher's lap. "My turn," she said, taking a deep breath.

"This Saturday I am getting married."

As soon as the class heard her news, everyone clapped.

Sidney whispered to Mary, "We knew it already!"

"Shhhh!" Mary scolded.

Sidney covered his mouth.

The teacher continued reading from her notebook.

"I'm very happy about that. It's going to be a special day. But there is something that will be very hard for me. My father will not be able to walk me down

the aisle. He is a major in the army overseas. He trains soldiers there. He won't be back for another year. I know my wedding will be fine, but I don't think I will be. I'll probably cry, and I want this to be a happy occasion. I'm trying to control my emotions, but it's hard for me to do."

When our teacher finished, it was very quiet.

Harry leaned forward and lowered his eyebrows. He looked worried. "If your dad isn't walking you down the aisle, who is?" he asked.

"No one. Mark and I don't have any brothers."

"Why can't you walk down with your mother?" Ida asked.

"Mom needs to stay with my grand-mother in the front row. She's very old."

Harry slowly sat up and crooked his arm. Then he started nodding.

Uh-oh! What was Harry thinking now?

Harry's Horrible Plan

At lunch, we talked about Miss Mackle's wedding in the cafeteria while Harry and ZuZu were in the hot lunch line getting tacos.

"I was hoping Miss Mackle might use an Elvis song in her wedding," Dexter said, waving his cheese stick in the air. "'Love Me Tender' would be perfect. Now I'll never know."

"Well, I'm crushed," Mary replied,

chomping into her tuna sandwich. "I wish I had written about how it feels not to get an invitation to your favorite teacher's wedding. Maybe Miss Mackle would have changed her mind and invited us."

"Hey, guys! Why the gloom and doom?" Harry said, joining our table. "I know how we can go to the wedding."

Song Lee stopped eating her strawberry yogurt. "How?" she asked.

Harry explained, "Doug's mom needs help making flower bouquets on Saturday at their church. We can do that, then just before noon, we leave. As we exit the church . . . we make a little sneaky stopover and spy on the wedding!"

"We can't do that, Harry!" Mary objected. "We'll get in big trouble. I know! My uncle is a policeman. He had to take some teenagers down to the station for disturbing a wedding. We'd be wedding crashers just like them!"

"Not crashers. Spies! Wedding spies," Harry explained.

"It's the same thing!" Mary replied.

"No it isn't," Harry insisted. "Spying

is sneaky and quiet. No one knows you're there."

"But what if someone sees you spying?" Ida asked.

"The only way it would work is if we had a good hiding place to spy from," ZuZu suggested.

"Yeah, a secret stakeout," Dexter added. "That would be way cool!"

"Doesn't your church have a balcony, Doug?" Harry asked with his mouth full of beef.

"Yeah, on the second floor."

"Great! We hide up there and look over the ledge. No one will see us. It's a perfect spy plan!"

"Doesn't sound bad, Harry," Dexter said.

"I like hiding," Sidney chimed in.

Mary dabbed her lips with a pink napkin. "I can't believe you guys are considering this! It's a dumb plan!"

Harry wouldn't give up. "Those flower bouquets are probably for some kind of charity. It's good to do something for others."

"We could just go and help Doug's mom," Song Lee said. "That would be nice. And maybe we'd even hear the music from Miss Mackle's wedding."

"We couldn't get in trouble for that," Ida agreed.

"Of course not!" Harry answered. "And when it's time, whoever wants to be a wedding spy can sneak up into the balcony with me. I'll stay up there with you guys . . . until twelve o'clock."

Everyone put down what they were eating and stared at Harry.

"What do you mean 'until twelve o'clock'?" I repeated. "Where are you going then?"

Harry popped the rest of his taco into his mouth. When he talked, there was red sauce dripping down the sides of his chin. "I'm walking our teacher down the aisle."

Mary's eyes bulged!

Song Lee and Ida gasped.

The rest of us froze.

"Harry!" Mary exclaimed. "You're not even invited! You can't just show up and escort the bride down the aisle! Besides, Miss Mackle plans to do it herself. You'd be disrupting her wedding!"

"Don't try to talk me out of it!" Harry said firmly. "I've made up my mind, and it's final. Miss Mackle needs a strong arm!" Then he crooked his right elbow, picked up his lunch tray, and marched over to the hot lunch line for seconds.

Mary rolled her eyes. "He's even practicing the part! Now we have to be wedding spies with Harry," she said. "It's an emergency! We must stop Harry from messing up Miss Mackle's wedding!"

"How do we stop him?" ZuZu asked.

"We'll think of something," Mary said. "In the meantime, we just have to stick with him!"

"Like glue," Sidney replied. When he tapped his fingers together, Mary did the same thing.

"This finger tapping," she said, "will be our secret reminder to keep a close eye on Harry at all times!" When she tapped her fingers again, we did, too.

As soon as Harry returned with another taco, he took a quick vote. "Okay guys, who's with me on Saturday?"

All of us raised our hands.

"Neato! Here's the plan." Harry lowered his voice. "We meet in the cemetery behind the Maplewood Church at exactly eleven o'clock on Saturday. We go in together, arrange some flower bouquets, then make our way up the stairway to the balcony. It's just a small family wedding. Everyone will be in the front pews facing the other way. We'll have ringside seats in that balcony, and a bird's-eye view."

ZuZu put two thumbs up!

"As soon as the church bell rings

twelve times for twelve o'clock, I'll dash downstairs to the lobby and offer Miss Mackle my arm."

When Harry crooked his elbow again, Mary groaned.

"Just remember!" Harry added. "This is top secret! Don't mention our wedding spy plan to anyone."

We all nodded in agreement.

Harry had no idea we had two secret plans—his plan to walk Miss Mackle down the aisle, and our plan to stop him!

The Church Cemetery

Saturday morning Harry and I rode our bikes over to the church cemetery. It was only two blocks from my house. Harry had his hair combed and was wearing a white dress shirt. I could tell he wanted to look nice when he walked our teacher down the aisle. Both of his pockets bulged, but I didn't ask what was in them.

As soon as we made a right turn

onto Maplewood, Harry raced down the street. It was like church row on that block. There were four churches right next to each other.

When Harry took a left into our church parking lot, there were only a few cars. Miss Mackle's wedding was still an hour away. I recognized Mom's station wagon with scratches on the fender. My brother, Baxter, did that

with his little steel car. I followed Harry as he rode to the back and parked at the cemetery gate.

Mary was already waiting for us under the gate with her hands on her hips. She was all dressed up in a fancy pink dress.

"This place gives me the creeps," Mary complained. "Why did you have us meet here, Harry, and not in the driveway?"

Harry flashed a toothy smile. "So we could read the gravestones while we're waiting for everyone to show up. Look at this one! It's really old!"

Harry and I bent over and tried to read the faded numerals.

"Oh good!" Mary said. "Sidney, Ida, and Song Lee are coming up the sidewalk!"

As soon as they saw Mary waving, the three of them ran over to the cemetery.

"You look so pretty," Song Lee said to Mary.

"This cemetery gives me the willies!" Sid exclaimed. "I'm not going inside."

"Me either," Mary said.

Ida and Song Lee apparently didn't have any willies. They joined us. "Look! Someone left roses on this grave!" Song Lee said.

Mary turned around and slowly walked into the cemetery. She wanted to see the flowers. "Someone must have just put them there. They're still fresh."

"Look at the name on the tombstone!" Ida called out.

We all did. "Fritz Birnbotham!"

"Mrs. Birnbotham goes to our church," I said with a shiver.

Everyone made a face. Mrs. Birnbotham was the strictest substitute teacher we ever had!

Just then, the bell tower began to chime eleven o'clock. *Bong! Bong! Bong!*

Dexter and ZuZu came running up the parking lot and into the cemetery. They were out of breath when they got to us.

Bong! Bong! Bong!

"My guitar lesson is usually over by ten thirty," Dexter explained. "Sorry, guys!"

"You're right on time, man," Harry replied, checking his watch. "Let's go! The sooner we make a few flower bouquets, the sooner we can get to our hideout in the balcony!"

Mary immediately tapped her fingers together. She was reminding us about our mission—stopping Harry!

Flower Baskets

When we got to the side entrance of the church, I opened the door.

"Cool!" Dexter said as we went downstairs into a dark, narrow hall.

"A secret passageway!" Harry exclaimed. "Is this the door we take to go upstairs?"

"Yes. That blue one. The first floor is where Miss Mackle's wedding will be. Second is the balcony. There's only about twenty stairs. Not high at all."

Harry very slowly opened the blue door and took a peak at the winding steps behind it. "I can do two floors," he said.

When we walked out of the narrow hallway and turned into Fellowship Hall, we could see Mom working at a far table with another lady. The table next to them had neat piles of artificial flowers and greenery, and a tall stack of small baskets.

"Hi, kids!" Mom called out. "Come on over!"

The girls immediately examined all the different flowers on the table— daisies, roses, lots of other kinds that I didn't have names for.

"Who gets these little baskets of flowers?" Ida asked.

"We're taking them to our local hospital. We hope to bring cheer to the patients," Mom said, smiling.

Song Lee clapped her hands.

Harry and I looked at our watches. It was five after eleven. We had plenty of time to fill a few baskets. We grabbed

handfuls of flowers and greenery and started stuffing one. The girls and Sidney took their time picking out things.

At eleven forty-five, Mom stood up. "My goodness, look at all the baskets you kids have made. There must be forty altogether now!"

The timing was perfect.

Harry immediately stood up, too. "Okay, guys, time for a break." Everyone quickly followed Harry's lead.

"Want to look around the cemetery for a while?" Mom asked. "I know Harry is interested in the gravestones."

"That's where we're headed!" Harry said.

As we hurried across Fellowship

Hall, my heart started to beat a little faster.

"Well, thank you very much, kids!" Mom called out. "Meet you back here!"

We all waved. We were now officially wedding spies!

Disaster in the Balcony

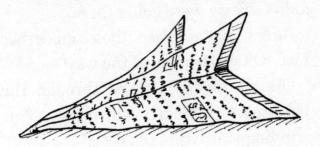

As soon as we got to the cloakroom, I grabbed the doorknob on the blue door. Harry held up a hand. We waited while he opened the other door to the parking lot, then slammed it shut.

"Now they'll think we went outside to play," he whispered.

"Did you have to lie about going to the cemetery?" Mary snapped.

"I didn't lie," Harry answered. "I

said we were headed for the cemetery. I didn't say we were going there."

Mary made a face, then zipped her lips. "Okay, Doug, lead the way!"

As we quietly tiptoed through the blue doorway, Dexter whispered, "This winding staircase is so cool!"

"Shhhh!" Mary shushed.

My heart was thumping loudly.

Harry was holding on to my shirt tail. When we got to the first floor, I

stopped. "This is the door to the church lobby. Don't touch it!"

Everyone nodded, then followed me up to the balcony. The seventh step creaked. I cringed when I stepped on it. I could hear seven more squeaks as my friends followed me up to the top.

"You okay, Harry?" I whispered.

"My mind's on Miss Mackle," he whispered back. "Keep going!"

When I got to the balcony door, I slowly turned the handle. "Kneel down," Harry whispered. "Walk on your knees, everyone."

Mary motioned to let Harry go ahead of me. When he was out in front, she whispered, "It will be easier to block him from leaving."

We nodded again, then dropped to

the floor and crawled to the first row, where Harry was squatting. There were only four sloping rows of pews.

"We're out of view now," Harry whispered. "And safe."

"But we have no view ourselves!" Sid complained. "Just the side of this short wall. When can we peek over the ledge, and spy on the wedding?"

"Not while I'm walking Miss Mackle

down the aisle!" Harry warned. "Everyone will be looking in your direction then. You guys can start spying when I get her to the altar." Then Harry whipped out a tie from one of his pockets and snapped it into place. "How do I look?" he asked Song Lee.

"Handsome." She giggled.

Mary made a face.

"How do we know when Miss Mackle gets to the altar if we don't take a peek?" Sid asked.

"We can tell when the wedding march stops," Ida answered. "That's what happened at my aunt's wedding."

"It's too hard to wait," Sid complained.

"Too bad," Mary scolded. Then she tapped her fingers together. She was reminding us why we were hiding with

Harry. We had to stop him from disrupting Miss Mackle's wedding!

Harry never noticed us tapping our fingers. He was taking a small pair of binoculars out of his other pocket.

"Can I borrow those?" Sid asked.

"Not now," Harry said. "You can use them when I leave."

"Boo." Sidney started to fuss.

Mary looked up at the pew behind her. Someone had left an old church program on the seat. "Here, Sid," she said. "You can make your own pair of binoculars. Just roll this up."

"All right!" Sidney took it and ripped apart the pages.

"Shhhhh!" we shushed.

Harry and I rechecked our watches. Eleven forty-seven. "Thirteen minutes to go!" Harry whispered, straightening his tie.

As we sat there silently crouching, the organist began playing a soft piece of music. We heard voices going up the aisle, people greeting each other, then lots of footsteps and the sounds of people sitting down. Three minutes later, Sidney showed Mary his finished art.

"Pretty good paper airplane, don't you think?" he bragged.

"I doubt that thing could fly," Mary said.

"Sure it can," replied Sidney. He stood up on his knees and sailed the plane forward.

All of us peeked over the ledge and watched it soar into the air. It was flying toward the altar of the church. We watched it slowly sway and sink from side to side, until it took a nosedive and landed in some lady's hat in the fourth row! When it dropped forward onto her lap, she turned around and looked up at the balcony.

It was Mrs. Birnbotham!

Now she was standing up, scowling!

All of us ducked!

Who would have guessed she was in the wedding family? I thought.

"Sidney!" Mary scolded. "I can't believe you did that!"

Sidney trembled. "I just wanted to show you it could fly! Do you think she saw us? Is Mrs. B-B-Birnbotham c-coming up h-here?"

Harry shushed both of them, then looked quickly around the balcony.

"If she finds us here, we're doomed!" Sid exclaimed.

The girls huddled together. Dexter clenched his teeth.

"Doug!" Harry whispered. "Is there any place we can hide up here?"

I pointed to a chain hanging down from the far ceiling in the corner behind a six-foot wall. "I could take you guys up to the belfry . . ."

"The belfry?" Sid said. "What's that?"

"The bell tower," I answered.

Harry looked at the goose pimples on his arm. "Here come the heebie-jeebies!" he said. "But there's no other way. Let's do it!"

Trapped in the Belfry

Harry crawled as fast as he could to the top row in the balcony. We followed, then crawled behind the divider wall. Very slowly I pulled down the chain. A climbing ladder of six wooden steps descended from the ceiling. It hardly made a noise. Harry scooted up the ladder right away. One by one we followed him.

As soon as Mary made it up into the

belfry, I pulled on the top stair with both hands. The climbing ladder automatically folded back into the ceiling. Quickly I locked it with a latch from the inside.

We all sat down silently on the wooden floor in the belfry and looked up high. The sunlight poured in between the wooden slats of the steeple. One giant church bell was directly above us. It was made of cast bronze and weighed four hundred pounds!

"You can see the sidewalk and street," Dexter said, turning around and peering between two slats.

"Shhh!" Mary snapped. "Someone could be coming any minute!"

Harry didn't turn around. He was petrified. I noticed little balls of sweat dripping down the sides of his face.

Suddenly, we heard a loud creak from that seventh step on the balcony stairway. Then a second creak. My heart was beating faster than ever!

"Two people are coming!" Mary whispered, putting a finger to her lip. Everyone else did the same. Even Sidney. Nobody moved.

A few seconds later, the balcony door opened. We could hear a woman's voice. "I thought the paper airplane came from here," she said sternly, "but I can't be sure. I didn't have my glasses on."

A male voice responded. "No one's here, Mrs. Birnbotham," he said.

Then we heard the door to the balcony close.

When Mary took a deep breath, we all did too.

"Phew!" we said, standing up.

Suddenly, Sidney jumped into Mary's arms. "What's that thing behind me!"

We all turned around and looked. Even Harry.

I laughed. "Don't worry, Sid," I said. "It's a wooden owl. Mom and I put it there last summer to keep the birds out of the belfry."

Harry patted its head. "This critter is the king of spies! He watches day and night."

Mary rolled her eyes, then pushed Sidney away. "Let's get out of this creepy place before that giant bell starts ringing."

Sid jumped up and covered his ears. "Oh no! The noise is going to blow my brains out!" Sidney rushed for the door. He tried to unlatch the lock in the wall to let the stairs down, but it was too tricky. He couldn't do it.

"I'll get it," I said. "Mom had to show me how."

I unclicked the latch and pushed the bottom step of the climbing ladder downward. I could hear the organ playing a new hymn as I watched the ladder slowly descend to the balcony floor below.

"Go down quickly!" Mary ordered

Sidney, Song Lee, Ida, Dexter, and ZuZu.

Harry was still next to that owl, but now he was looking between the wooden slats with his binoculars.

Mary hurried down the climbing steps. As soon as she got to the balcony floor below, she whispered a command. "Doug, pull this up now! Lock yourself in the belfry with Harry. It's the only way we can really stop him from spoiling Miss Mackle's wedding!"

Whoa, I thought. Can I do that to Harry?

Suddenly, the big brass bell began to ring right over my head . . .

The Wedding Surprise

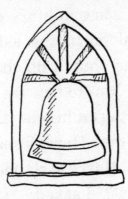

*B*ONG! *BONG! BONG!*

The ringing was louder than thunder. It was a horrible noise! I had to cover my ears as the bell chimed twelve o'clock. When I looked at Harry, he was adjusting his binoculars.

"Don't your ears hurt?"

"Noise doesn't bother me!" Harry replied. "But my stomach does. It's spinning now."

"What are you looking at?" I asked.

"There's some military guy wandering up and down the sidewalk. He's going to the church up the street. I'm waiting for him to face me so I can see that name tag on his chest."

I looked over Harry's shoulder.

"Got it!!" Harry exclaimed.

"Got what?" I asked.

Harry ignored my question. "It's time

to go!" he said. Then he pushed me aside and scooted down the steps of the climbing ladder. When he landed on the balcony floor, he made a mad dash for the exit.

Mary looked frantic. "Doug! You have to catch him!"

I knew that for sure! I took off after Harry. I was right on his heels as he raced down the stairs.

When we burst into the lobby, Miss Mackle was forming a line with her maid of honor and two bridesmaids "Harry! Doug! What are you doing here?" our teacher said.

At that moment, the organist started playing a trumpet introduction. The usher motioned for the bridesmaids to start walking.

"Don't go yet, Miss Mackle!" Harry pleaded. Then, he dashed outside the double doors of the church. I followed him across the lawn and onto the sidewalk. That soldier was about to enter the church two doors down.

Harry shouted to him. "MAJOR MACKLE! OVER HERE!"

Major Mackle? Huh? I thought.

The man dressed in a military uniform with lots of medals quickly turned around. As soon as we met up, Harry took him with us. We raced back across the lawn and up the steps. Just as we opened the double doors to the church, we could see the maid of honor making her trip down the aisle. No one else was in the lobby but the bride.

"Dad!" Miss Mackle called out.

She dropped her bouquet and ran into his arms.

"You made it to my wedding!"

"I wanted to surprise you, Piglet. I just got a little lost."

Miss Mackle and her father shared a long hug.

Then she turned around and slipped

her arm into her father's. "This is the best day of my life!" she exclaimed.

"Well, you have these boys to thank. They rescued me just in time. I was headed for the wrong church down the street. There must be three weddings going on today!"

"Harry spotted your father with his binoculars from the belfry," I said.

"Thank you, Harry," Miss Mackle said, half laughing. "You boys be sure to sit in on my wedding, okay?"

"Fantastic!" Harry replied, picking up our teacher's bouquet and handing it to her. "But there are a few more of us." And he ran upstairs to get the others.

Mary, Song Lee, Ida, Sidney, Dexter, and ZuZu came down in a flash.

Mary curtsied as soon as she saw the bride with her father.

Song Lee and Ida *ooh*ed and *ahh*ed when they saw the crown of daisies in Miss Mackle's hair.

"Please go in, kids," she said. "I want you all to be a part of this too now!"

As we hurried down the aisle, Harry made a point of sitting right behind Mrs. Birnbotham.

When she turned around, she was scowling. "Were you the rascal who flew that airplane?"

Harry shook his head. "No, ma'am. I don't have a pilot's license."

When I started giggling, Mrs. Birnbotham made a face. She didn't stop
glaring at us until the organist began
playing the wedding march.

Everyone stood up and faced the
back of the church.

I elbowed Harry to look upstairs at
the balcony. My mother was peeking
around the door!

"Awesome! Your mom's a spy, too,"
Harry said.

Finally, Miss Mackle made her way
down the aisle on the arm of her father.
We couldn't help but hum along:

> *Dum, dum, dah dummm,*
> *Dum, dum, dah dummm,*
> *Dum, dum, dah, dum, dum,*
> *Dah dum, dum, dah dum.*

"I love her dress!" Song Lee said.

"I love her wedding bouquet!" Ida added.

"Those are white stargazers!" Mary said. "They smell divine!"

The groom waited at the altar in a dark suit with a daisy in his buttonhole.

A vase of yellow and white flowers sat at the altar next to the American flag.

All four rows of people had their eyes on the bride. Some were crying.

When Miss Mackle passed us and got to the first row, she paused for a moment, while Major Mackle hugged his wife. Miss Mackle's mom was crying. She seemed surprised to see Major Mackle, too.

As the minister greeted them at the

altar, Major Mackle stepped back and stood with his wife in the first row. The groom took his place next to our teacher. The minister began speaking. "Who gives this bride to be married today?"

Major Mackle stepped forward. "Her mother and I."

The reverend asked the couple to repeat a lot of words, then he said to the groom, "Now you may kiss your bride."

Mary and Ida and Song Lee leaned forward to get a better view.

ZuZu and I exchanged a look. The kiss took too long.

Mary giggled. "We're watching the best part!" she said, clasping her hands together.

Harry and Dexter seemed to agree with Mary. "That kiss seals the deal," Harry said.

"It's important," Dexter added.

"Shhhh!" Mrs. Birnbotham replied, this time glaring at us over her glasses.

Miss Mackle and her new husband turned around and walked back up the aisle, arm in arm. When they got closer, she looked over and waved. "Thank you, Harry!" she whispered.

Harry beamed.

As soon as she passed us, Mary tapped Harry on his shoulder. "I'm sorry about asking Doug to lock you in the belfry," she said. "That was a horrible thing to do, especially when you're afraid of heights. I just didn't want you spoiling our teacher's wedding!"

Harry shrugged. "I didn't even know you said that, Mare. I was busy spying with that wooden owl. He was the one who really helped me get through my heebie-jeebies. I figured if he could spend ten months in that belfry, I could at least spend a few more minutes."

"Well, you did a good thing, Harry," she said. "You got Miss Mackle's father to the wedding just in time!"

"Thanks to my friend in the belfry,"
Harry replied. "Owl sure miss him."
Mary sighed. "Oh, puhleese, Harry!"